WELCOME TO
PASSPORT TO READING
A beginning reader's ticket to a brand-new world!

Every book in this program is designed to build read-along and read-alone skills, level by level, through engaging and enriching stories. As the reader turns each page, he or she will become more confident with new vocabulary, sight words, and comprehension.

These PASSPORT TO READING levels will help you choose the perfect book for every reader.

READING TOGETHER
Read short words in simple sentence structures together to begin a reader's journey.

READING OUT LOUD
Encourage developing readers to sound out words in more complex stories with simple vocabulary.

READING INDEPENDENTLY
Newly independent readers gain confidence reading more complex sentences with higher word counts.

READY TO READ MORE
Readers prepare for chapter books with fewer illustrations and longer paragraphs.

This book features sight words from the educator-supported Dolch Sight Words List. This encourages the reader to recognize commonly used vocabulary words, increasing reading speed and fluency.

For more information, please visit passporttoreadingbooks.com.

Enjoy the journey!

Little, Brown and Company

Hachette Book Group
1290 Avenue of the Americas, New York, NY 10104
Visit us at lb-kids.com

Little, Brown and Company is a division of Hachette Book Group, Inc. The Little, Brown name and logo are trademarks of Hachette Book Group, Inc.

The publisher is not responsible for websites (or their content) that are not owned by the publisher.

First Edition: September 2016

Library of Congress Control Number: 2016935540

ISBN: 978-0-316-27441-8

10 9 8 7 6 5 4 3 2 1

CW

Printed in the United States of America

Licensed By:

Meet Blurr

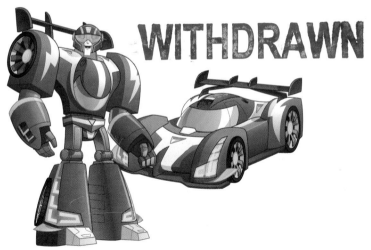

WITHDRAWN

Adapted by **Steve Foxe**

Based on the episodes
"Rescue Bots Academy" written by
Zac Atkinson

and "A New Hero" written by
Marty Isenberg

LITTLE, BROWN AND COMPANY
New York Boston

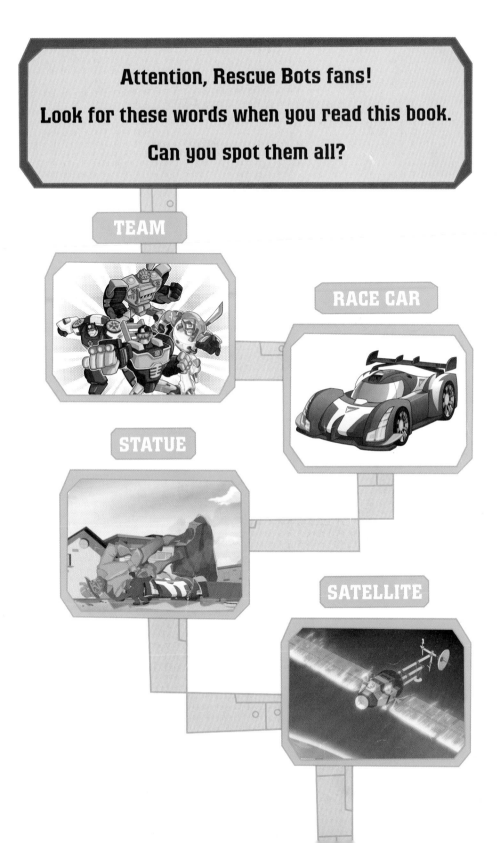

Attention, Rescue Bots fans!

Look for these words when you read this book.

Can you spot them all?

TEAM

RACE CAR

STATUE

SATELLITE

The Rescue Bots
are on a special mission
from Optimus Prime
to serve and protect humans.

Heatwave is their leader.
Chase, Boulder, and Blades
are on the team.

Two new Autobots have arrived!
Salvage turns into a garbage truck.
He is quiet and friendly.

Blurr turns into a race car.

ZOOM!

Blurr is always in a hurry.

He only looks out for himself.

The Rescue Bots
teach Salvage and Blurr
how to work with others
as part of a team.

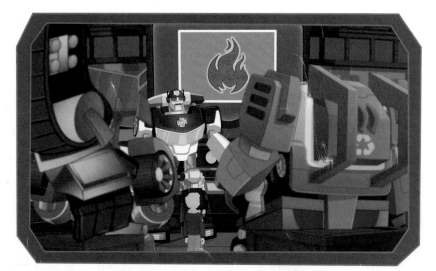

Blurr fails the training session.

He will not admit he was wrong.

Heatwave is not sure Blurr

is cut out to be a Rescue Bot.

Cody believes in Blurr.

Cody has an idea.

"Salvage and Blurr should attend
Rescue Bots Academy," he says.

Salvage is a great student.

Blurr is not.

The Rescue Bots get a call.

Someone is in danger downtown!

Cody asks Heatwave

to give the new Bots a chance to help.

A window washer is trapped up high.

Blurr rushes in.

He bumps the platform on accident.

The man falls off!

15

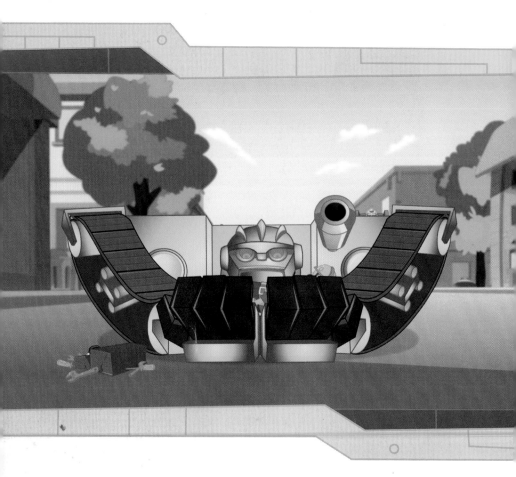

Boulder catches the man just in time.
"We are supposed to put safety first,"
Kade says to Blurr.

Back at the firehouse,
Heatwave is upset with Blurr.
"You are too reckless," he says.

Blurr is in a bad mood.

He goes for a drive to clear his mind.

But he races too fast.

CRASH!

Blurr knocks over a statue!

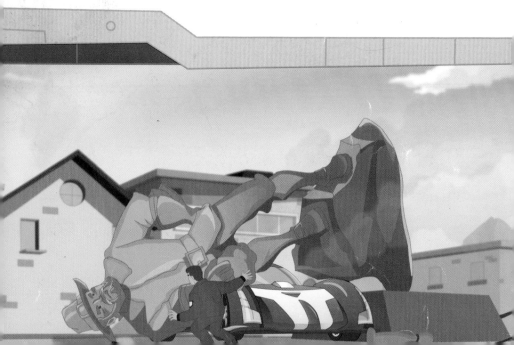

Heatwave has had enough.

Blurr hears him talking to Optimus Prime.

"I have made up my mind," Heatwave says.

"Blurr has got to go."

"We finally agree on something,"
Blurr thinks to himself.
He decides to take a spaceship
and leave Earth.

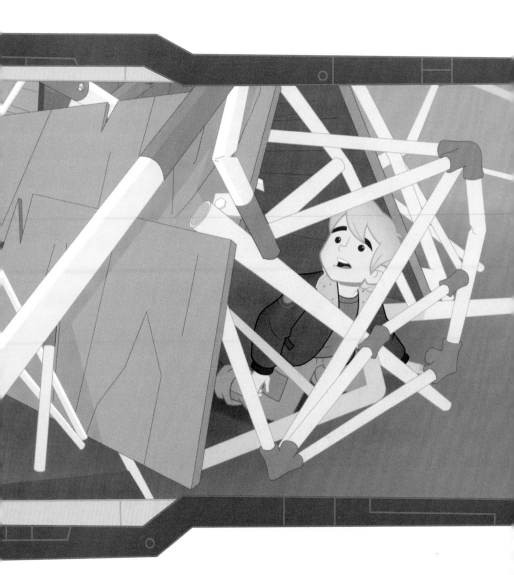

The hangar shakes when the
spaceship takes off.
A bunch of metal falls.
Cody is trapped underneath it!

Cody whistles for help.

Servo the robot dog leads

the Rescue Bots to the hangar!

They save Cody.

But there is another problem.

Solar flares are hitting the island
and knocking out all electronics!
The Rescue Bots are too busy
to chase after Blurr.

The Rescue Bots spring into action.

Blades helps land a plane.

Salvage guides a boat to shore.

Doc Greene spots a bigger problem.

A solar flare broke a satellite.

Now it is falling.

It is headed straight for Griffin Rock!

The spaceship tells Blurr
about the falling satellite.

"It is not my problem," Blurr says.

The Autobot remembers
that Cody believes in him.
"On second thought,
turn the ship around."

Blurr aims the ship's lasers at the satellite.

But they are not working!

"Even when I try to do the right thing,
I mess up," he says.

"We can help!" Salvage says
over the radio.
The Autobots on Earth
help Blurr turn on the laser.

Blurr has to fly close to the satellite.

It is very dangerous!

He aims the laser and fires.

Blurr saves the day!

"I was wrong about you,"

Heatwave says.

Optimus agrees.

He asks Blurr and Salvage

to start a new team of Rescue Bots!

Blurr thanks Cody for believing in him.

"You helped me," he says.

Cody is sad to see Blurr leave.

"We go where we are needed," Blurr says.

"We are Rescue Bots!"